THE SEA IS BLUE

ALSO BY MARIE A. LAWSON:

DRAGON JOHN

THE SEA IS BLUE

WRITTEN AND ILLUSTRATED BY

MARIE A. LAWSON

THE JUNIOR LITERARY GUILD
AND
THE VIKING PRESS
NEW YORK 1946

621

IN MEMORY
OF · A · SAILOR
L · B · H

CONTENTS

THE SEA IS BLUE

CHAPTER ONE

TIMMY

Timothy Daniel Burney was, on the whole, very happy. He had no father and no mother, but he had never had them, save so briefly, and had been without them so long, it was all very vague and dim.

He remembered his mother mostly as a bewitching smell of lavender, and his father, chiefly, as a smell of salt water and oilskins, and a voice—a deep, singing, ringing voice, like the sound of the sea off the great point of rocks beyond the harbor.

True, when he passed certain gardens, say, on a hot day in August—and took a deep breath in, he would have a queer little twinge near his heart, and, when the wind was just a certain way and the sea had that deep-throated, talking sound, he would sigh.

But he loved Uncle Captain Burney with so absorbing a passion, and he so loved the little house they lived in, with its ship's clock with its bells that were such good company; with its great cobwebs of nets and of tackle, its mysterious charts, its compasses, that most of the time he was not lonely or forlorn at all.

Besides, he had a boat all his own. It was small, and he could sail only a very short way, and then he must obediently come back to the safety of the familiar brown wharves, with their crusts of barnacles and waving seaweed. And only in fair, calm weather could he go at all. But it was sailing, and he could, when alone, talk. Talk loud and gruff, like Uncle Captain and the other fishermen; and, by and by, even that was not enough. And he got to be a pirate captain, with a crew of forty, or fifty, or even a hundred, and, those times, he talked very loud indeed.

But all this was for fair days alone—summer days mostly. That left all winter and part of the spring and a great deal of the autumn.

For eight weary months he studied with the minister, Parson Meigs, and he didn't like it. Somehow, *threes* and *fours* and *A*'s and *B*'s simply meant nothing

at all. And he didn't like the Parson's house; it was so depressingly full of books: brown books like the rocks he was told never to sail near, grayish books like fog, and black books like night time. And, there were, also, other children. Children worried him a lot; he couldn't understand why, when there were so many of them, so very, very few were quite right for friends. They were either older, or too much younger, or else just not the right kind.

Two years ago school had been better, when Scrubs and Freckles, who belonged to Mr. Martin, the shipyard man, had been there. They had been older, but somehow it hadn't mattered. But now Scrubs was a big, almost grown man, and a fisherman himself, and Freckles, who was just turned fourteen, was working in the shipyard, with its sweet smell of shavings, its spicy tang of tar and resin, its cheery music of hammers. And Timmy missed them woefully.

He just couldn't like the rest of them. There was the minister's brood, of course: Joshua and Saul, and Faith, Hope, and Charity, all older, and Abimelech, who was five whole months younger than Timmy but discouragingly, disgustingly bright. All of them wore round glasses that made them look like owls. Timmy could never imagine them tucked cozily in bed, under the comfort of warm patchwork quilts; he always saw them, in his mind, seated in a row on a tree limb at night, beginning with the tallness of Joshua and ending with the smallness of Abimelech, and reciting on and on . . .

"Water," Joshua would hoot solemnly, "is part hydrogen and part oxygen. . . ." (How silly! Why even he, Timmy, knew it was the harbor out there, blue and sparkling, with white, wheeling gulls above and silver fish below.)

Then Saul would screech forth all the English kings without a single mistake. Faith, Hope, and Charity would chirp, smugly, in one, two, three order, and, at the last, would come a little shrill squeaking from Abimelech.

Then there was Archibald Unwin, who was ever so spindly and scrubbed, and, being brought up by a widowed mother and three black-silk aunts, knew nothing of boats or sails or nets, and, what was worse, didn't seem to care. In fact, he was perfectly useless save for his amazing skill at adding two eggs to nine eggs, and never once hastily saying a dozen, or subtracting three pieces of toffee from eight pieces, and never once thinking, or apparently even hoping, that six—a round, comfortable half dozen—were left.

And there were the Hammett twins, Cornelia and
Cordelia, who looked exactly like the china dolls in
Mrs. Smith's store, with their round blue eyes and
round pink cheeks and round heads with round scal-
lops of framing hair. What with their looking so alike
and their names so near the same even poor Mr. Meigs
would sometimes get them mixed up. They always
said "Good Morning" to Timmy, very politely, and
he always made a point of saying two separate "Good
Mornings" in return, but he had given up, long ago,
trying to tell which was which.

And there was Cecilia Winfield. She really bothered
him more than all the rest of the children put together.

If she had been ten or six or even nine or seven, he
would never have thought of her at all, but she was
just his age, eight; to be exact, she was eight and three
days when he was eight without so much as an hour
extra.

But Cecilia was out of the question. She was bright and beautiful and rich and gay, and—it might as well be said—very content with herself. She gave Timmy a brief nod each morning, and then presumably forgot all about him. Never once, when the blessed release from lessons came, had she asked him to go home with her to the big house with the tall white pillars and the flowery garden, and the big, jolly Negro butler and the hall with its twinkling chandeliers. Archibald went often, Abimelech now and again, and the twins a lot.

Only one time had Timmy gone there at all, and that was to her birthday party last year. She hadn't asked him to that; Mrs. Winfield had sent word by Uncle Captain. Timmy had gone, all trembly and eager, and had come home laden with little baskets of candy and with a real orange, and very full of cake, but he had not had a good time. There had been so many city cousins and friends, all dressed up and using words he didn't know, and even Archibald and Abimelech and the twins, whom he saw daily, looked like strangers in their party clothes.

The very second Cecilia had greeted him, though ever so politely, with her frilly white dress and her blue sash, like a big butterfly, and her curls all shiny gold, he had suddenly felt awkward and grubby. He could imagine how red and shaggy his hair looked— just like Mr. McKinloch's old sheep dog—and his freckles fairly burnt millions of prickly hot holes in his face.

So this year, this very day it was, he just hadn't gone. He felt very bad about it because Uncle Captain had made a tiny boat, with the smallest of fish nets and oars, all complete, for him to take as a present. But he simply couldn't go.

That night, just as he was closing the door of his small bedroom, he had heard Uncle Captain talking to Mr. Martin, the shipbuilder, and had caught his own name.

"A funny child," he had said, and it was the first time he had ever felt even a wee scrap of a hurt feeling with Uncle Captain. The rest was beyond him:

". . . maybe he'll be a sailor, or maybe a poet, or mayhap just one of the world's vagabonds, but, whichever he is, he'll likely be all three."

And a rumble of laughter and a whiff of pipe smoke drifted upward. Oh, oh, he hadn't meant to listen at all; he closed the door softly.

But how could one person be three, and what was a world's vagabond? A poet wrote things; that was clearly out of his line. Even gentle Mr. Meigs had been almost impatient today when Timmy made a whole row of *s*'s backward, and had somehow twisted the tails of his *y*'s so that they all looked like *if*'s.

Besides, he had long, long ago decided to be a sailor . . . the very first time he remembered seeing a white sail fill with wind; even before that . . . when he was very little and had held Grandpa Bent's big pink shell to his ear and heard the sea roaring inside.

He almost felt a tear coming, as he thought of all the children he didn't like or who didn't like him, and of Uncle Captain thinking him funny, but it dried right up when he realized Uncle Captain must really like him to be so good to him—and when he remembered all his older friends.

He sat up in bed so he could count them on his fingers against the space of moonlit night framed by his window, and, having counted, snuggled down under his quilt to think about them.

CHAPTER TWO

A HOST OF FRIENDS

First, there was Grandpa Bent, whose cottage had a brass door knocker shaped like an anchor, and beyond the door was a treasure house of bits of sweet-smelling wood, spools of fine, strong flax thread, and glue pots and paint pots and tiny brushes. Grandpa made models of ships these days, but he had been a great sea captain—"a deep sea sailor," he said—to whom this big harbor was no more than a "little lake." In all the Seven Seas he had been; "up and down, and round about" he had.

And, besides the big table, with its models and tools, there were more treasures all over the house: pink shells from an island beach "somewhere south," the gleaming polished whales' teeth on the mantel shelf, fat little carved figures from "somewhere east," shiny black boxes delicately painted with strange houses and queer people and twisty trees and funny boats, and a red chest carved with a fearsome dragon that had an almost endless, twisty, twiny tail.

Yes, and besides all these there was a slipper of blue satin, embroidered with birds and blossoms and butter-flies. It was so small not even Cecilia Winfield could have gotten her foot into it, but Grandpa Bent had assured him it had fitted a grown lady in China, full twenty years old.

And there was Miss Effie, who lived, all by her lone, in a house as big as Cecilia's. All alone, save for Sarah and Seth, who were servants, and lots of clocks and lots of china. Everywhere were china figures: ladies and gentlemen, and smug, spotty dogs, and lambs lying on green bases, starred with flowers.

Timmy liked the clocks best—the tall one in the hall, with the deep voice, and the sun and moon on its face, the tinkly-sweet one in the parlor, but, best of all, the one where a little door flew open and out popped a bird, who sang as many cuckoos as the hour it was and then popped in again and shut the door

behind it. "Does it ever make a mistake, Miss Effie?" asked Timmy shyly.

"It never has."

Timmy sighed, and after that he always called the cuckoo Archibald in his mind, but he didn't tell Miss Effie, for fear she already had a name of her own.

It was here he had his first cup of tea, mostly milk, out of a blue and white cup called "Willow Pattern." It had a picture-story all over it, of two devoted lovers who ran away from an angry father, and Miss Effie hadn't minded one bit when he tipped half his tea on the rug, so excited he was to see if they really escaped on the far side of the cup.

And there was Mr. Martin, at the shipyard, who always saved scraps of most beautiful lumber for the making of toy boats. Here he could watch Freckles at work, and see a whole ship grow—from the first great bare ribs of her to the final, strong, rounded, slim body, with its intricate pattern of rigging. Here, in the sail lofts, he could see ells and ells of lifeless canvas cut and sewn into odd shapes, so soon to be transformed into those wind-filled wings beating south, north, west, east—all up and down and round about Grandpa Bent's own Seven Seas.

And there was Mr. Cather and his tiny shop where

he sold spicy buns and gingerbread monkeys, and sticks of hard, sharp, sweet candy.

Mr. Cather always played a game. If Timmy could guess what flavor stick he held, in each hand, behind his back, he got two for a penny instead of one. Somehow, Timmy always did. He couldn't understand it, and Mr. Cather couldn't explain it—save that Timmy must have been born under a lucky star!

Often and often he wondered which was his star, craning his tousled head out of his little window, gazing at all the millions of bright dots in the dark heavens. He felt he should at least wave to his star and say thank you, but there was no way to pick it out. Mr. Cather had no idea, nor Uncle Captain, nor even Grandpa Bent.

And there were Mr. and Mrs. O'Brian, who used to ask Uncle Captain and Timmy to supper ever so often. When he was very young there had been a high chair at the table for him—painted green, save right on the front rung where it was worn down to the warm brown wood. Mr. and Mrs. O'Brian had told him exactly opposite things about the color of the chair when he admired it.

" 'T is the color of the sea, far out," Mr. O'Brian had said.

But Mrs. O'Brian had spoken quick and sharp.

"Ah, no, no, 't is the color of the dear, sweet land, the color of the green fields of Ireland, Timmy, where I lived when I was as young as you!"

He had always wondered, with no children in the house, or even a mention of grown-up ones, why the little chair was there. And why, when he had grown so he could scarce squeeze into it, Mrs. O'Brian had sighed. And why, once, when he had eaten his supper and couldn't get out, and had to be pulled and pried loose by Mr. O'Brian and Uncle Captain, she had really cried.

And there was "Big Barney," the blacksmith, with his cheery bright forge and ringing anvil, and "Little Barney," his son, who was so tall he had to stoop to go in his own front door. Whenever Timmy was about he would lift him on the back of some huge horse and give him a ride, all down the lane and back.

There was old McKinloch, with his rough-haired, friendly big dog. Although he lived way out on the moors, McKinloch never failed to appear in the blustery, pale spring to take Timmy out to see the new baby lambs, with their wool like snow, and their wobbly legs and twitchy noses, looking for all the world as if they had been dipped in fireplace soot.

There were, also, the Vosborgs, who lived on a real farm miles from town, and were foreign folk from far across the sea. Before he met them, Timmy had expected them to be a different color from himself, and have maybe four legs and more than one head. He was truly surprised when they turned out to be like everyone else, save for a funny way of talking.

Ever so often, when Farmer Vosborg came into town, he would take Timmy out for a visit.

The days at the Vosborgs varied with the seasons. In the spring there were countless new animals to admire: shy, leggy colts, soft-muzzled calves, puff balls of golden chicks, wee pink satin pigs, plush puppies, velvet kittens.

It was in spring, too, that Timmy always played his special, secret game: to the top of the tallest tree he would climb and, hidden in the branches, make believe he was in the crow's-nest of a tossing whaler— —the lookout. He pretended the rolling green pastures were the sea, the drifts of pear tree blossoms "white water," and that enormous back, which was really Farmer Vosborg's pet horse, old Thor, was the hump of a whale. Much as he liked all the Vosborg children, large and small, this game he kept to himself.

Summer brought the joys of hayrides and picnics, and then, all sweetly hot and sticky, swims in the clear river; autumn, the friendly rivalry of finding the most nuts, the largest pumpkin, the first red ear of corn; and

winter, the mysterious silence of snow, the roaring hearth fires, the bounteous dishes of steamy, savory food.

"Man's food," would bellow Farmer Vosborg, with relish, "man's food, to make little men into big ones!"

Then Timmy would eat and eat and always hope, come morning, he'd waken to find himself as big as Farmer Vosborg and Uncle Captain and "Little Barney" all rolled into one.

Part of his homecoming was the solemn ceremony of being measured by Uncle Captain, and never had he failed to grow a bit, but, unfortunately, it was often round about instead of up and down.

Even better than the delightful days at the farm,

Timmy loved the nights. They were always the same, whether the family gathered under the fragrant canopy of fruit trees, or before the flaming, crackling fireplace. It was then that tall Svend would play tunes on his fiddle, some hauntingly sad, some dancing merry.

And Christel would tell stories and sing songs, in her own tongue. But always, most carefully and kindly, she told Timmy what they were about. . . .

Of the squat dwarfs in hidden mountain caves who forged silver horseshoes and golden bracelets and swords a king would envy; of elf maidens, dangerously fair, who lured away many a lone shepherd and hunter. . . .

But, best of all, of the long-ago sea kings of her country, who, with nought but the shining stars to guide them, in open galleys braved the tumult of the northern seas. Of Eric the Red, who found the far-off isle of Greenland, and when Eric aged and his hands faltered on the great tiller, sent his son, Leif, still farther—all the way to America.

"Five hundred years before the Italian gentleman came," Christel would end proudly.

"I think," Christel said once, gazing into Timmy's

wide, eager eyes, "that the Sea King, from his name, must have had red, red hair. Like yours."

"Not like mine?" cried Timmy in astonishment, "surely not like mine?"

Gently, Christel ruffled the rough red curls.

"Exactly," said she, gravely.

After that, he never minded his hair so much. . . .

There was also Miss Mollie, the dearest of all.

Long before Timmy was born, her father, Captain Dane, had owned a whole fleet of ships—the pride of the town, everyone said. Once upon a time, Captain Dane (a stout, hearty man he was then) had sailed away in the finest and newest ship of all, and been shipwrecked. Years after he had come home, all skinny and old, with a long white beard and hair, and had gone into his great brick house with the wall for good and all. And Miss Mollie with him. She hadn't come out till she came with the coffin that held the old Captain, twenty years later.

Strange tales were whispered about the old man—of how he'd sing weird songs in foreign tongues, of how sometimes he knew Miss Mollie and sometimes not, and some days he laughed the day long and sometimes he wept.

Now Miss Mollie lived in a little house out where the moors began, with its back turned square to the sea.

"And not a window seaside, neither," had said Grandpa Bent. "Very sad," he added. And Miss Effie had said the selfsame thing.

But Timmy didn't think Miss Mollie was sad at all; the garden was gay and the house was gay and Miss Mollie was gay. She was always making bright quilts and sparkling jellies, and bags of lavender and herbs and tiny jars of potpourri. There were dozens of shiny copper kettles, and always bowls of flowers, and a cheery, trilling canary; even her cat was gayer patterned than most, with patches of ink black and bright orange and snowy white. Miss Mollie herself wore green and blue and pink and lavender and yellow dresses, and her hair was soft brown, and her eyes were twinkling greeny brown, like river water.

And, oh, the smell of that house! Of ginger and roses, and lavender and cinnamon and strawberry jam!

Often Timmy used to gather berries and plums for her. He was always glad of an excuse to go there; to open the white gate, to tread carefully the sanded walk between the nodding flowers, to lift the polished

knocker, and to hear Miss Mollie's light step running to answer.

There was something odd about Miss Mollie's step; it had a dance in it—it sounded young.

Thinking of all these things, Timmy grew drowsier and drowsier, almost forgetting about Uncle Captain's calling him "funny"; about the hind-part-before *s*'s and the wrong-side-to tailed *y*'s; about Archibald and Abimelech and Cecilia's birthday party.

He could almost smell Miss Mollie's kitchen, and just as he dozed off he could almost hear Christel singing—or was it the chimes in the church tower, or only the sea?

Anyway, it didn't matter . . . the song was about Eric the Sea King, plunging courageously through towering waves, his red hair blazing in the sun, blowing in the sea wind.

"Just like mine," he muttered, burrowing his red head deeper into the pillow.

"Yes," sang Christel and the chimes and the sea, "red, red, red, just like yours, exactly."

CHAPTER THREE

SUPPER FOR THREE

Timmy's days varied no end—black days, medium days, red-letter days. School was always a burden, and there were extra lonely times when Uncle Captain was kept late fishing and could not return for sunset and supper. But visits were always red-letter days, and he always had the secret comfort of the far-off, long-ago, red-haired Sea King.

But there came a morning when everything was wrong. He woke to a howling gale and sluicing rain. He had planned many things for the day, for Mr. Meigs was away and there was no school. But, when he stumbled downstairs, still half asleep, Uncle

Captain was gulping his breakfast and his oilskins lay ready on a chair.

"Timmy," he said, "there's a boat wrecked at the point . . . we are going out . . . I may be very late—maybe tomorrow."

Timmy gazed at the hard rain beating on the window panes; afar off he could hear the sea pounding, crashing. An icy fear struck at his heart; he swallowed uncomfortably.

Uncle Captain pulled on his oilskins. For a second he held Timmy close.

"I'm disappointed, too, Timmy," he said, gruffly. "I had hoped to be home with you today. But we must go. There are men out there needing help; it's a heavy sea."

Timmy swallowed again, but the lump in his throat was too big to talk through.

"Timmy, Timmy," said Uncle Captain, "you are warm and safe here in the house; if you are afraid of the loneliness and the storms, you will never be a sail—" He bit his lip and stopped.

"Why, oh, why," he muttered, as he fought his way to the wharves against the rain and wind, "did I say 'sailor'?"

When, in the last hour she lived, Timmy's own

mother had begged him to keep her son from the sea! To send him to school, to fit him for any profession —anything but the sea.

And his brother, Timothy—what had he wanted? There had been no time to ask; the sea had been Timothy's life—and Timothy's death. Would he want his son . . . ?

Captain Burney clenched his gnarled hands; willingly, gladly, he had given up the long sea roads he loved, to stay home and be a fisherman and take care of Timothy's son. If only he could do the right thing.

But, now, the thinking must wait. He was in the old green dory, with the salt spray all but blinding him. He threw up his head for the fight; no boat could last long on those rocks, no man in such icy waters.

~~~~~

Timmy didn't find the day so bad, or the first part of the evening. As long as the light held, he worked on a boat he had started, and he made up a long story about sailing her east, where dwelt the great red dragon and the lovely Chinese ladies with their tiny feet; then south, where he built himself a whole castle of sea shells, with the pink inside, so there was always a sunset glow over everything. And then his stomach suddenly told him it was suppertime.

He decided to ask Eric and the Chinese lady (he didn't ask the dragon, not being sure what it ate), and they all supped happily together on kippered herring and cambric tea, and the one cooky left from those Miss Mollie had given him the day before and a partly sucked peppermint stick from Mr. Cather's.

But after supper things were not so good; Eric just wouldn't stay, and the Chinese lady looked so very out of place in this windswept, storm-beaten house that soon she too was gone.

And Timmy was all alone—dismally alone.

He could not know that Uncle Captain had been stopped, as he bent his head against the storm that morning, with a dozen offers to take him, Timmy, for the night. Or that Uncle Captain had laughed in utter scorn.

"My brother's son afraid of the dark, or a storm! Never!"

He could not know that Miss Mollie, with tears in her eyes, was peering toward his house through the blinding rain on her window panes.

Or that Cecilia's mother had tried to send Cecilia's father to get him, and that once Mr. Winfield had got as far as his own front door. And then stopped.

"It's useless, Amy," he said, for the tenth time,

"you know Dan Burney, and you knew Timothy, and you know Timmy—the little beggar wouldn't stir; he's a sailor's son, grandson, and on, since time began, and redheaded to boot. He's probably sound asleep, and dreaming he's Christopher Columbus or Francis Drake this minute."

Timmy knew none of this; only that he ached with loneliness, that the familiar fishing nets had become cobwebs of horror, that the storm seemed to be beating into his brain, and that, for the first time in his life, he was desperately afraid. Not for himself, but for Uncle Captain.

Uncle Captain didn't know how much Timmy had learned, of late, about the sea and ships.

Uncle Captain had never talked much about it; he treated it just as a matter of course—down to the wharves and out in the green dory, and when there was plenty of fish he was glad, and when there was not, he'd sigh a bit. Just like Farmer Vosborg, driving his great horses out of the barn each morning, across the green acres, and when there was a fine harvest he was all smiles, and when it wouldn't rain and the crops dried up, he would look, for him, very grave.

But from Grandpa Bent he had gathered another

idea about the sea: of the beauty and the glory of it —the immense, beckoning expanse, with its tumbling whitecaps, "the noble white horses"; of the vessels themselves, with their sheer splendor of raking mast and singing rigging; of the fabulous lands beyond the rim; of the priceless cargoes—precious furs and shimmering silks, the sheen of ivory, the gleam of pearls.

Until the last year, this and this only had been his sea: the familiar routine of Uncle Captain's fishing, the glamorous horizons of Grandpa Bent.

But now there was something new about the sea —vague but terrible.

Sitting, mouse-quiet and unnoticed, he had heard talk here and there—in the shipyard, in Barney's forge, in shops.

He had learned that Farmer Vosborg had had two sons, older and taller than Svend, and that they had bade good-by to the golden hayfields and gone forth upon the sea—and—had not come back. He remembered how eagerly Svend and Farmer Vosborg used to question him about every ship that came into the harbor; how Christel's voice, when she sang certain songs, would catch in her throat.

He had heard more of Miss Mollie, too; of how,

when the sea sent back her father, no longer a strong man but an ailing child, and she had shut herself up in the walled house to care for him, she had also given up her lover, and the beautiful wedding that was all planned, even down to the white satin slippers for Miss Mollie's dancing feet.

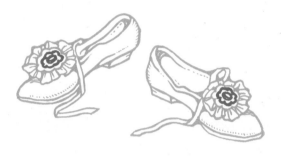

He had found out about the green high chair at the O'Brians; that long ago there had been babies there, and then big boys and grown men; that all of them had been sailors—and—none had ever come back.

And once his ears had caught his own name, Timothy, and then he realized that it was only his name and not himself, but Timothy his father. Timothy, who, on just such a night as this, when there seemed no battling the sea's fury and the wind's anger, had gone forth to a call for help. Somehow he had brought back five living men in a leaking, battered boat, only to die, his hands still clenched upon the oars, at the very wharves of home.

All these dire and bitter things the sea had done . . . and now Uncle Captain was out there. . . .

The clock struck eight bells—four o'clock in the morning. Mercifully, Timmy fell asleep, and slept all around the clock.

When he finally woke and ran outside, the sun was breaking the mist into long white streamers, and, reaching in a mighty arch between the sea and heaven, was a band of color—of all colors, shimmering, delicate, wonderful.

Even as he stared, came the crunch of heavy boots, and he was in Uncle Captain's arms, burrowing his face in the familiar, smelly oilskins, and, to his utter dismay and shame, crying.

Uncle Captain had never known Timmy to cry; he was astonished and somewhat at a loss. Clumsily he lifted Timmy high in his strong arms, and pointed to the great bow.

"Rainbow," he said, "the rain is past, the storm is over, and now the crying must stop!"

Just then the rainbow faded into gray mist, and Timmy, clinging to the wet oilskin shoulder, wept anew.

But when Uncle Captain demanded a reason, he just couldn't bring himself to tell of his long night, so he blamed the rainbow.

"I didn't want it to go away," he sobbed.

It was after supper that Uncle Captain told him about the game. He had been thinking a lot—all the time he was brewing tea and cutting bread and gnawing cheese and having his after-supper smoke.

"Timmy," he said at last, "the rainbow never lasts long. It's one of those lovely things you see, for the space of a breath, and then it's gone. When I was your age—and I guess a lot older, too—I had a game I made up. I used to make rainbows out of everything I saw —a color here, another there. I remember my mother used to be very proud about how good and quiet I was in church, when most young ones were a-squirming and a-dozing through the Parson's long sermons. Well, as a matter of fact, I was making rainbows; the stained glass windows had about every color in them, and you never knew what Sunday a lady would have a new dress or bonnet, or a little girl a new sash."

He stared fixedly at the fire. But he wasn't seeing the fire at all, just now, but a garden, gay with yellow and orange flowers, with towering green trees with long violet shadows under them, and a glimpse of blue sea beyond, and a slim girl in a gay red gown.

"For instance, Timmy . . ." and then he told him about the rainbow in his memory. Timmy carefully counted all the colors, on one hand and one thumb extra—red, orange, yellow, green, blue, and violet.

"Oh, Uncle Captain, what a beautiful one! And did it go all of a sudden, too?"

"It did, Tim, all of a sudden and forever."

"But couldn't you make another?"

"We-l-l, someway I didn't then, and now I'm out of practice and a trifle old. But you could make 'em; there's really no end to what you can find . . . rising suns and daffydills and . . . look at the fire, Timmy, there's yellow and orange and red right there, all in a heap—and, here, let's throw on a bit of driftwood. I'd not be surprised if the sea salt on it wouldn't give us a blue flame for the harbor, and the green of deep water beyond, and maybe even the purply violet shadow that falls on a white sail along toward sunset. There, what did I tell you?—every one of them! And now off to bed with ye!"

CHAPTER FOUR

TEA FOR TWO

Timmy was late for school next morning on account of the red for his rainbow; he went the long way round to get the Fallons' red barn. He had selected orange marigolds from Miss Mollie's garden, the trees were still green, the sea was blue as blue today, and he'd met old Mrs. Jermyn (a stroke of luck that was) with a violet bow on her bonnet. Now the yellow— well, he just couldn't be any later; he'd have to get his yellow after school. But there, as he entered the schoolroom, sat Cecilia, by the window, and her hair was as yellow as any sunrise in the world!

School seemed endless that day, he was so eager to be out and about and begin a new rainbow.

He was leaning on the gate of the parsonage, trying to decide which way to take home, when Cecilia came out. Miss Uppity-up, he thought, gleefully, how cross she'd be if she knew I had her hair! He was so pleased with the idea he quite forgot he hated her, and smiled. The smile was not really for Cecilia but at her, but since she didn't know that she stopped.

"If you'll walk home with me," she said, "we can have cambric tea and ginger cookies."

His heart gave a funny little jump, but this time he didn't want to go, and there was a sort of queenly air about her invitation he didn't like.

I'm Timothy's son, he thought—the second Timothy—and I have the same color hair as a great Sea King, and who is she? She might even be one of those dangerous elf-maids Christel told about, so strangely fair she was.

So he merely said, very offhand, "Sorry, but I can't go that way, and, besides, I'm very busy."

Cecilia was astounded.

"But—but—you're only leaning on the gate; I can see you, perfectly plain."

Oh, could she? The awkward, shabby body of him, yes, but not the Timmy who made rainbows all his own.

And suddenly remembering he could start a whole new rainbow with Miss Mollie's canary, he turned and walked away.

Cecilia, with tears misting her eyes, stood very still where he had left her.

~~~~~

He felt he should explain to Miss Mollie before he took the color of her canary. Miss Mollie was always just exactly right about everything. She said she was not only pleased, but very, very proud to have her canary used in the rainbow, and then she gave him a fat little jar of orange marmalade for orange as well as to eat later for supper. She had on a green dress that day, too.

Then, not wanting to take too much from Miss Mollie in one day, he went over to Grandpa Bent's and got his red from the dragon chest, and his blue from the Chinese lady's slipper. Then he raced over to Mrs. O'Brian's to look at her purple asters before it got dark.

Oh, what a game this was! What a glorious game!

He burst in upon Uncle Captain, breathless and beaming.

All through the golden autumn Timmy was in high spirits, with this delightful secret hugged to his heart. Red and orange and yellow were easy these days, with the leaves turning and chrysanthemums in bloom. The sky was mostly blue, and when it rained he could always fall back on Uncle Captain's eyes. He had been hard put to it for violet, though, with the asters over and old Mrs. Jermyn laid up with rheumatism.

Then one morning in school he looked up suddenly and saw Cecilia staring at him, very hard and straight. And he saw that her eyes were the color of pansies, blue violet, deep and dark.

It was the very day he noticed this that Cecilia called to him just as he reached the gate. It was the first time she had spoken since that other time; she had even stopped nodding mornings.

Because he felt a little guilty about taking her eyes and hair without her knowing, he stopped.

"Timmy"—she wasn't queenly today, but oddly pink and stammery—"will you come to tea with me this afternoon?"

He really didn't want to. He had been playing his game so much and so long he couldn't bear to stop, and things were getting harder this last week, with the gardens all frosted and the trees bare. That was why he had been forced to use Cecilia's eyes today; twice last week he had had to use a patch from Miss Mollie's cat; once, even his own hair for red.

"Wouldn't you rather have Archibald or Abimelech or the twins?"

"No," said Cecilia decidedly, "I would not. The twins just want to roll dolls in carriages, up and down, up and down, or else put them to bed, or something dull like that. And Archibald is so solemn and afraid of dirt and Abimelech reads all the time and looks at ants and bugs with a funny glass which makes them look huge and horrid. I—I'm really very lonesome."

Cecilia lonesome! This was a new idea. Cecilia, with her curls and her big house and jolly Caesar, the butler, and all her toys and a father and a mother!

"All right," he said, and then he had to think a second . . . "thank you for your kind invitation."

The tea was very good, and the ginger cookies crisp and buttery, and it was queer and exciting to have Caesar pass him cream and sugar on a shining silver tray, but he couldn't think of much to say, and he had to keep thinking of the Sea King, Eric, to keep up his courage.

Then in came Cecilia's mother wearing a blue dress, and a shawl all patterned in orange and purple and red, and, when she held out her hand to greet Timmy, there on her white finger was a flashing green stone, set in gold.

"Oh, oh, oh," cried Timmy, "you have all the colors, all at once, you're a whole—" and then he stopped short and turned so red even his freckles didn't show. He wished he could sink through the floor, through the dark cellar, through the earth below, all the way to where Grandpa Bent said China was.

But Mrs. Winfield only smiled and looked a little puzzled, and then went away, her skirts rustling like leaves, leaving behind her a faint fragrance like—like —springtime.

But Cecilia had noticed.

"Whatever did you mean, Timmy? A whole what?"

He was so wretched he had to tell her; after all, he had stolen her hair and her eyes, and been rude about coming to tea, and left a sentence to her mother right halfway in the middle of the air.

So he poured out the whole story, right from the beginning. Cecilia sat very still, her pansy eyes round and serious. Timmy feared she might laugh, but she didn't, not even about using her hair for the first rainbow, or having to take a patch from Miss Mollie's cat twice in one week.

When he stopped, quite out of breath, she only said, 'How beautiful, Timmy," and tried to smile while two big tears rolled down and into her teacup.

The next morning, just as Timmy was getting up, he saw the back of big Caesar going down their path, and when he came to breakfast Uncle Captain handed him a small envelope. Timmy had never had a letter in his life, so he waited till after breakfast to open it.

Dear Timmy:

I want to make rainbows. But if you don't want me to, I won't. But if you don't mind, we could take a walk this afternoon and make one apiece and not tell what till tea time.

Cecilia Winfield.

P. S.   I will never tell anybody, anyway.

But somehow they had to talk some about it.

"Cecilia, are you using the sky or the sea for blue? I'll take whichever you don't want."

"Neither, and I wish you'd call me Cissy—it's much more friendly."

"I will, I'd like it—but they are the only two blues I see anywheres."

"Well, I've got another. You can't see it now, but I'll show you when we get home."

This was both perplexing and annoying.

"Then," said Timmy, "you started at home ahead of when I got there." That's what comes of playing a game with a girl, he thought to himself grimly.

"I did not," was the quick retort, "I can see the blue now—right now."

When teatime came she led him to the long gilt mirror in the hall.

"There's my blue," she said, in triumph, "your own eyes; you took colors off me when I wasn't even in on the secret, so now I've taken your eyes for blue, and your hair for red, and your freckles for orange— they really are, you know, and there was yellow paint on one of your hands and green on the other—"

"I was painting my little boats this morning," said Timmy, ruefully.

"So," she went on, "I admit I was almost through the second you came—*not before*—except for a violet."

"I haven't a violet now," said Timmy. "I didn't like to take your eyes again so soon. Wherever did you find it, Cissy?"

"Just as we came in the gate I saw that shadow on the snow under the big elm. Look out the window— it's as violet as violets themselves."

So Cissy won, and Timmy was surprised that he didn't mind a bit.

Spring seemed to come in no time that year. Timmy was allowed to work a little in the shipyard during the summer. What with this, and sailing, and Cissy added to his list of friends, the summer was gone like a single day.

Another spring, another, and another.

The last time Uncle Captain had measured Timmy he had whistled a long, low whistle.

"You're growing up and down now, Timmy, not just round about!"

He took down a battered ledger, and put on his spectacles.

"I got a few accounts to do, Timmy . . . "

"All right, I'm going down to help Freckles a while."

Uncle Captain stared, unseeing, at the open ledger. The time must come, and very soon, for some decision.

CHAPTER FIVE

A PROMISE OF PEARLS

"I can't see you today, Cissy," said Timmy firmly. "You really take up no end of time. I don't mean I don't like it, but it's been weeks since I went to see Grandpa Bent or Miss Mollie or anybody."

"Couldn't I go with you?"

"Why, yes, Cissy, if you'd like it—of course they are all much older than you."

Cecilia's temper flared.

"And how about you, Timothy Daniel Burney? I'm three days older than you are this minute! And I always will be. There's no way in the world you can catch up—Father said so!"

"Well," said Timmy meekly, "let's begin with Grandpa Bent."

Grandpa Bent was delighted to see them. Before they left he hobbled to a cupboard and took down a small box Timmy had never seen before. From layer upon layer of crumpled paper he took two little packets. One he gave to Cissy to take home; it was a tiny Chinese doll, dressed in gold brocade and it even had slippers, all embroidered like the real one Grandpa Bent had. The other package he unwrapped on his

work table, and there, in the sunlight, lay a string of beads, which were really white, but, oh, miracle, indeed, shone with all the colors of the rainbow, blue in one light, yellow in another . . . .

"And these," said Grandpa Bent, dropping them into Cissy's hand, "will be yours when, and *if*, you marry the right man. You'll get them the very day I hear the good word, and I'll—" he chuckled—"I'll dance at your wedding!"

Cissy held the pearls tenderly in her small pink palm.

"Could you give me any hints at all, Grandpa Bent, about the right man? For I'd love to have the beautiful beads, and I'm sure I'd admire your dancing."

Grandpa Bent eyed her solemnly over his glasses.

"Well, first and last, Miss, he *must* be a sailor—a big man and a brave one. He must sail all the Seven Seas same as I did, and—he must—dream dreams!"

When they had gone he pushed aside all the bits of wood and tools and paint pots and glue pots and, taking the Chinese lady's little slipper from its box, set it on the table before him. For a long time he sat looking at it through the haze of his pipe smoke. After a while he didn't see either the table or the slipper but long, long swells of water—the Pacific—and overhead great billows of white canvas, high white clouds of sail—and then the greenery of land and drifts of flowering trees and red and gold tiptilted pagodas gleaming in the sunset. In his ears he heard the deep kling-klang of temple bells and the sound of a lute and a woman's voice, and the slowest of small, oh, very small footsteps coming nearer—nearer. . . .

Then they were suddenly big footsteps, very real, and a big fist on his door, and it was none other than Uncle Captain Dan Burney himself, come for a pipe or two and a chat. By the look of him, a very serious chat, indeed.

And so it was.

Uncle Captain, when he talked to Grandpa Bent, nearly always began in the middle. But Grandpa

Bent, except when he was contrary and didn't want to, always understood.

"He is near twelve years old," said Uncle Captain. "Now what on earth can I do?"

"Dan," said Grandpa Bent, "no matter what you do, the story will have the same ending."

"But," said Uncle Captain, "his mother begged me, and Farmer Vosborg and poor Norah O'Brian and Mr. Winfield all say send him away to school—inland—and I understand Miss Mollie says—of course I've not seen her," he added hastily.

He relit his pipe and puffed hard, his brow wrinkling.

"His mother, Ellen," he went on, "she loved books and poetry and such like, and though Timmy is powerful slow in school, he does think some and has a touch of poetry in him. I don't rightly know what his father would want; it's different, you know, loving the sea yourself, and wanting your baby—your one son . . . it was a hard death, Pop Bent."

Grandpa Bent laid a hand over the big brown one clenched on the table.

"I know, Dan," he said gently. "I know. But you'll have to follow your own feelings. Seeing the way I do, I'd say put the boy in the shipyards a while, and then—well, if he's going to learn and to dream dreams, he'll dream 'em at sea, and a lot more like to than stuffed up in some college on the land. But I don't know, Dan; I can't help you. And the boy himself?"

Uncle Captain sighed.

"I've been trying to find something might interest him. You know how girls count buttons on their dresses to see who they'll marry? Well, I've just about gone through the list, leaving out beggarman and thief, and of course Indian chief, that being out of the question.

"There's rich man, poor man, and he don't care which, and doctor, which means nothing with him never sick a day in his life, and lawyer, and he'd never make out at that, with his simple, straight ways of thinking. I left out soldier on account of its having sailor right next word, and I've forgot a few, but I'm sure there is one line has 'merchant prince' in it. And that seemed the best. There's Burr Adair, up to Salem, you know, what was Timothy's good friend and is also mine, and he'd take Timmy on, in the warehouses, and, if he works, later on in the offices. With some more schooling, of course. First, the boy has to learn to add a simple sum in less'n two hours,

and write less like a cat in a fit, and some mite of navigation, so as to plan routes. Adair has a great lot of ships, and no son to aid him."

Grandpa Bent took the crumpled letter Uncle Captain held out, and took a long time reading it.

"I think," he said slowly, "you've struck the very thing."

Uncle Captain beamed.

"I think so. Timmy was dead set against more school, but he mostly minds what I say. You see," he went on, "I figured this way—that at Adair's he could see the ships coming and going, and smell the tar and the salt, and write down the lists, and figure things about the cargoes, and, if he saves, someday he might have his own ships, and enjoy watching 'em built and sending 'em forth, without actually sailing 'em, and then he'd be a 'merchant prince,' in a manner of speaking, and well content."

"Exactly so," said Grandpa Bent, "and very, very clever of you to figure it out, Dan. Wait a minute, I'll hold the door open till you get down the path. It's right dark tonight. I wish Timmy luck, and you, too."

He watched Uncle Captain's broad back down the path, listened to his heavy, retreating footsteps.

"You blessed old idiot," he murmured, "watching the ships—smelling the tar and the salt, huh! And content!"

He closed the door softly, and laughed, long and loud and hearty. And went to bed fairly cackling.

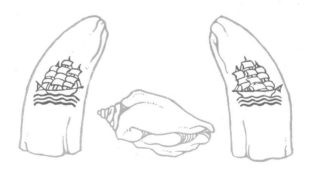

CHAPTER SIX

LETTERS

"I still," said Timmy, on the very wharves, "would rather not go. I could help you fish and work in the shipyard, and, a little later, get a place as cabin boy. I could now; after all, I am twelve. Almost."

But he stopped at the sight of Uncle Captain's face.

"I'll do the best I can, and—you'll let me come home for the summer?" he finished miserably.

"If I can afford it, Timmy; if the fish run well. If not you better study this summer, so's to go to Mr. Adair's sooner."

And so Timmy went.

"If I let him come home, I'll never get him off

again," muttered Uncle Captain, turning away when he could no longer see even a speck of the little boat on the horizon.

"And I must—I must try."

Timmy was utterly miserable for months and months. He had to swallow a big lump in his throat a good part of the time, and there was a woeful lack of rainbows. He had promised one to Cissy, but it was a long time before she got it. When Caesar brought her the fat envelope, at last, she took two of her father's biggest handkerchiefs, and climbed up to the attic, to be all alone.

The letter wasn't as long as the envelope was fat, for Timmy still wrote pretty large and sprawling.

Dear Cissy
     It has snowed most of the time and there seemed

to be no color at all. And I wished I was home, so I could run to Miss Effie's for a scrap of blue from the Willer Patten plates, and to Grandpa Bent's for a sight of the red dragon chest, and to Miss Mollie's for a bit of orange off her cat. And every time I would get so homesick I couldn't write at all. But, come dusk yesterday, I started seeing things again. The bildings what are just gray stone turned a nice blue, and the red brick ones violet, and folks started lighting candles and they shone through the windows, all yeller and warm like. And I took a walk and found a little forrest of brite green pines and one lone holly tree with red berries. And, on the way home, I saw a stripy orange cat in front of the butcher man's. So here's my rainbow for this time.

And please Cissy, send me one soon. And, even if we have used them a lot before, send me your eyes and hair for part of it, because I miss you terrible.

I'm getting on fine with arithmetick now I use it in the carpentry class—it just made no sence before. And I like geogriffy. I've found all the Seven Seas Grandpa Bent talks about, and I learned a lot more by accydent while I was hunting them. The worst things now are littratuer and spelling.

Give my love to everybody you know I like, and tell me what folks are doing.

Timmy

Don't forget my rainbow, please. And soon.

But it was some weeks before he got it. It was spring. Her eyes and her hair, three fat green cater-pillars on one leaf, an orange bowl from Miss Mollie's, blue scillas from her own garden, and her red, well, it was something neither of them had ever had before —not apples or Barney's red shirt, or strawberry jam; it was such a surprise she had put it on a separate piece of paper, tightly folded into a little cocked hat. His hands shook so he could scarcely get it open:

Timmy, the youngest O'Brian boy came home!
! ! ! ! And his hair is redder than red—redder than
yours, even. And that's my red for this time. Mrs.
O'Brian cried and laughed and then began all over
again. And she had a party and even Grandpa Bent
came. And the O'Brian boy, who is really grown up,
and ever so big, tried to sit in your green high chair,
and everybody laughed some more, and Mrs.
O'Brian cried again. Timmy, you know I'm not
sure even the pearls Grandpa Bent promised me
would make it worth while to marry a sailor, with
him gone so long, and maybe always.

P.S. You shouldn't say you miss me "terrible";
it's really "terribly" and it would be more correct
if you said "miss you very much" or something like
that.

P.S. Again.
Try harder on the literature and spelling, Timmy,
and then maybe you'll be a poet and stay home under
a tree, with pen and ink and no danger.

Cissy

And, for the first time, Timmy realized how very
different were a boy and a girl. For who, who could
give up the sea road for a tree, who forsake the glory
of canvas and the beautiful lace of rigging for pen
and ink?

His next letter was very manlike and brief.

Cissy

I have been too busy studying to colleck a rainbow or even write.

Timmy

And then he relented a little and added a postscript.

P.S. When I said I missed you terrible, Cissy, it was terrible I meant. I'll say terribly sence you say its kerect, But I can't leave it at just "very much" because that's only a tenth of how much the miss was. Could I say dreadful, instead?

Uncle Captain had a letter, too.

Please, Uncle Captain, can't I come home this summer? And why don't you want me to go to sea? I've figured out you don't, but why?

Uncle Captain's answer wasn't a bit like Uncle Captain. He had been obliged to get Mr. Winfield to help him with it. It explained, most carefully and patiently, about how few boys ever had such a wonderful opportunity as Timmy did, to go to a fine school and be taken in by Mr. Adair, and all that. And no, he couldn't come home this summer, but likely next.

Cissy's next letter made him more homesick than ever.

Timmy, I decided to get a whole rainbow from Miss Mollie's because you always loved her house so. [Cissy must know he wasn't to come home, and was trying to comfort him.]

I counted on the canary to begin with, and he was gone. Miss Mollie says he's done it before, but he always comes back. But there we were, with no yellow. The daffodils and primroses were over. But Miss Mollie dug down in a little trunk and took out some slippers—pale yellow satin. She said she had them when she was a girl and that they were white when they were new. They looked so little and so kind of young I asked her if she'd ever danced in them, and she looked very funny and said she'd never worn them at all, and changed the subject real quick. Then we hunted in the garden for violets, and found just one, and I took a patch from the cat for orange, for I know you like him, blue from Miss Mollie's dress, and green from that leafy hooked rug in the hall. And then red, and that was just about hopeless. You remember we noticed Miss Mollie never had anything red, not even red flowers? Then she suddenly clapped her hands and said, "Oh, Cissy, your mouth—it's as red as cherries and we should have thought of it long before! So here it is, Timmy. It's not really from Miss Mollie's, as I planned, but it's there a great deal.

Write soon, please,

Cissy

Cissy's mouth—and all the many times he had seen it and never thought of stealing it for red! As if he were not feeling stupid enough today, for Mr. Matthews, the headmaster, had spoken to him about his literature again.

"But I won't need it," he had protested. "I'll only need spelling and writing and geography and figures —that's all I'll ever need at Mr. Adair's."

"But," said Mr. Matthews gently, "reading will help the spelling and the way you write things down, Timothy, and, who knows, one day you may be a rich man like Mr. Adair, and have to talk to all sorts of people, and you couldn't just say, 'Two dozen cases of tea,' or, 'Cape Horn is on the southern tip of South America.'"

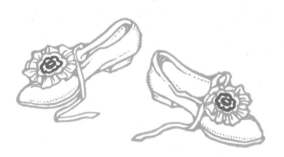

CHAPTER SEVEN

HIDDEN RAINBOWS

So here Timmy was, shut in Mr. Matthews' study, with Mr. Matthews' voice droning in his sleepy ears.

"You may read anything you choose, Timothy, but do try. Just take one book after another, and maybe you'll find something you like, after all."

He closed the door, quietly but firmly.

Timmy gazed out of the window at the pale spring sunshine. It made him sleepy to stay indoors; even sleepier to read. If only he were out today he might be able to collect a rainbow for Cissy, in answer to her perfect one. But how could he, shut in here? He glared around. Brown leather chairs, browny gray rugs, and those tons of books in their drab bindings.

Sighing heavily, he pulled down a few, and opened one at random. Something caught his eye.

> Fair daffodils, we weep to see
> You haste away so soon . . .

Miss Mollie always said the daffodils were too soon over. How often Cissy and he had started a rainbow with them! Yellow.

Impatiently he ruffled the pages.

> Tiger, tiger, burning bright
> In the forests of the night . . .

Orange.

Of course Timmy had never seen a tiger, but Grandpa Bent had, in one of his long-ago voyages East.

"A sort of oversize cat," he had said, "orange as fire flames and black stripes on it neat as if painted by Mr. Chew, what does the fancy trim on carriage wheels."

Hastily he thumbed the pages.

> I sometimes think that never blows so red
> The Rose as where some buried Caesar bled . . .

Why here, hidden under all this black and white print, were colors—pieces of rainbow!

Suppose, oh suppose, he could get a whole rainbow out of books! Surely, Cissy would be impressed!

He picked up another book.

> The blue of the unfathomed sea . . .

Blue.

He turned a few more pages.

> While proudly rising o'er the azure realm,
> In gallant trim the gilded vessel goes.

What a nice sound that had! He opened the big dictionary and searched diligently through the *a*'s. Yes, azure was blue, too.

Of course both he and Cissy had used the sea a hundred times for blue, but they had never called it "unfathomed," let alone "azure realm."

There still remained a green and a violet to be gotten. He found a lot of greens right off; these poet fellows talked no end about trees and meadows, but he wanted one he liked the sound of.

> The priests are on the ocean green,
> They march along the deep.

Green.

> There's wine from the royal Pope . . .

Now wine might be purple, like grapes, but it

might be red, or amber—orange, like Miss Mollie's beads. He'd look further; he wanted this rainbow to be just right.

He took down a small worn book, and, he could hardly believe his eyes, but there it was, printed out plain as plain could be:

> Her eyebrows in the willow he can trace,
> And silken pansies thrill him with her eyes.

Timmy sat quietly in the big leather chair; he had to think. He had always thought words were just words, hard to remember and to spell, and written down by gray old men, like Mr. Matthews and Parson Meigs, and people like that.

He must have been wrong. These folk must be young, to be putting scraps of rainbow in writing; some must even be sailors, to speak so often of the sea.

He bent over the little book lying open on the desk. He must find out about this last one—this boy who must have seen Cissy's eyes, discovered they looked like pansies, even knew how you felt when you looked at them.

Painstakingly, he read: "Po-Chui, Chinese poet, born 772 A.D." Why, he must be older than Grandpa

Bent—older than anybody—he must be—he must have lived a long, long time ago. It gave Timmy his first inkling of a great truth: that some things he thought were new were old; that some old things are ever new.

"Timothy," said Mr. Matthews, at the door, "I didn't mean you must stay in all afternoon—only a while . . ."

Timmy jumped.

"I found a lot of things," he stammered. He stared at the books again; no longer did they seem musty and fusty and drab.

"Would you let me come again? And, Mr. Matthews, could I take these books, just till to-morrow?"

"Of course," said Mr. Matthews, "and come as often as you like."

And Timmy, his eyes still wide, his mind awhirl, was gone.

Mr. Matthews, alone, stroked his chin.

"I do wonder," he said to himself, "what he found. I'd so like to be young again, if only for one after-noon."

Up in his little bare room, Timmy, by the light of a candle, labored long into the night.

He could hardly wait for Cissy's answer. It would have to be a pretty fat one to equal his last. But when it came, it was very thin.

Oh, Timmy, Timmy, your last rainbow was so beautiful I fear I can never come up to it. But I'll start making one now, slowly and carefully, and have it ready when you get home. You sound older, Timmy. Do you know yet what day you will come? I asked Captain Burney but he didn't seem to be sure when school let out.

Cissy

He wrote Uncle Captain that very day, and then, three days later, he wrote Cissy again.

I am not coming, Cissy. I am sorry.

The summer was long, but Timmy studied as he had never studied before. If he couldn't go home, then the sooner he could go to Mr. Adair's the better. There he'd be near ships again, and also he could earn a little money and not be a burden on Uncle Captain. Three times he had had to ask for clothes—he outgrew them so fast.

The next summer he didn't ask to come home; he went to Mr. Adair's. But Uncle Captain came to see him. All the little hurts faded away at the sight of

that familiar big bulk, at the love and pride in Uncle Captain's face.

"Mr. Adair says you are coming fine, Timmy. And you do like it?"

"Yes—" he hesitated—"of course."

And he did like it. It was great fun to see the ships going forth—to the world's end; to watch the great sails go up, the dripping anchors lift; to write down the beautiful names: *Pride of India,* bound for Calcutta; *Star of the East*, just in from Hong Kong; *The Southern Cross,* home from the Indies. He liked counting over the cargoes, too: the gay India prints, the multicolored shining silks, tea wrapped in gold and red papers, pungent bags of coffee beans, packets that held the sharp, sweet tang of spices and always made him think of Miss Mollie's sunlit kitchen.

All too soon Uncle Captain went home, and in no time another summer had come, and gone, and another and another and yet another.

Amid all this bustle of ships and cargo lists home seemed very far away. Uncle Captain sent occasional scrawls, months apart; baskets came every so often from Miss Mollie, bless her soul—baskets brimming over with cookies and jams and glistening marmalade. Christel wrote now and again; so did Cissy.

He seldom wrote to Cissy; he meant to, but the time got away so. Once in a while he sent a rainbow, when the ships came in. When they went out, he never could write at all—these were his bad days.

Mr. Adair was kind, very kind, and Timmy knew he was getting on—more and more left to his hands, fewer and fewer orders, higher pay.

But often, before a ship sailed, when he knew the crew slept, he would steal on board before dawn—to stand by the great wheel, to run his strong fingers lovingly over the smooth, worn wood of it—to gaze up and up, at the towering masts against the stars, at the folded wings of the sails, quiet now, but to-morrow—yes, these were the bad times.

It was after such a night as this that he had a letter from Cissy.

Dear Timmy,

Do you realize it's been years and years since I saw you? Are you very big? Captain Burney says you are, but I still think of you as you went away, so young and forlorn.

Abimelech came from college last week; he's going to be a scientist—bugs and things like that. He's shut in the house now; got in a hornet's nest the very day he came home. Archibald is at home too. He's grown quite tall, Timmy, but still spindly.

He's much taken with one of the twins, but he can't really tell them apart, even yet, so whichever one wants to go out with him, goes. Miss Mollie is just the same, and so is Grandpa Bent. I think Michael O'Brian, for his mother's sake, will stay home. He's fishing now.

I went to my first dance (first real grown-up one) last night; Mother let me tuck up my hair and have a new long dress—it's the color of lilacs.

You've not sent a rainbow in ages, Timmy. Is there any chance of your coming home this summer?

Cissy

Timmy gazed out of his window. Across the way lilac bushes were all abloom in a little garden. There was a bed of nodding yellow tulips, with a border of pansies. A strange, hard lump seemed to be caught in his throat.

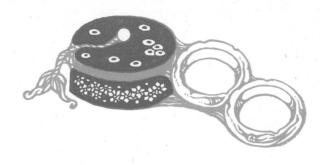

CHAPTER EIGHT

CISSY BECOMES CECILIA

When Timmy, with some hesitation, asked for a bit of leave, Mr. Adair hadn't minded a bit; thought it high time for a vacation. But would Uncle Captain mind, when he hadn't asked permission, but just written he was coming? Would Uncle Captain meet him? And Cissy?

Leaning over the rail, Timmy's thoughts were all in a jumble; the swishing water below, lilac bloom, white foam curling backward, the salt wind in his face, Miss Mollie's kitchen—he hadn't realized how much he had longed for home. Oh, there it was, looking like a toy town in the distance, its houses curving around the blue harbor. Ten minutes more, five, three, one—they were almost in—he heard the creaking of anchor chains.

Hands were waving. There was Uncle Captain! And the Martins, and the O'Brians, tall Svend Vosborg and Christel, Miss Effie, and Seth, laden with her shawls and parasol, Mr. Winfield and Caesar, and oh, even Grandpa Bent!

What a homecoming! Everyone talking at once, and Timmy with only two hands to go around among them all. And, could it be—was this little Cissy, this whirlwind of long, billowing skirts and flying feet?

She stopped, breathless, a foot away from him.

"I—I—didn't expect you to be quite so big," she stammered, and then turned very pink under her blue bonnet, and held out a hand in a lace mitt. "How do you do, Timothy," she said, "it's so very, very nice to see you."

That was the way she was all the time he was home. He simply couldn't get used to her. He hated her long skirts and her bonnets and her tucked-up curls.

He had brought her jade bracelets Captain Alan

had bought for him in China, and, when he gave them to her, that first evening, he had said, "Green, Cissy, green."

She had opened the box with cries of delight, had called her father and mother to see them, and had worn them every time he had seen her, but—she hadn't gone on with any more colors.

She must have outgrown rainbows, all of a sudden, thought Timmy bitterly. And afterward he was terrible—no, terribly—ashamed lest she had thought him childish.

When she asked him to tea, it was always a party, with Archibald, the twins, Abimelech, looking more like an owl than ever, and, often, her house-party guests, and even strangers who had moved to town since he left. And Michael O'Brian, who was really very nice, but whom Timmy resented because he was a smidge taller and a lot older and had been a real sure-enough sailor.

Just one walk he had with Cissy alone, and she had suggested that. It was a very silent walk. When they came to Miss Mollie's he almost said, "The canary is yellow, Cissy," but, stealing a glance at the top of her prim little bonnet, he didn't.

He did not see her quick, shy glance up at his red

head, so tall above her, did not see her mouth open
and close again.

She called him Timothy now, so he called her
Cecilia.

But everything else was all right; it was good to be
with Uncle Captain in the little house with the fishing nets, to wander in the shipyards, to visit with all
his old friends.

He loved to sit in Miss Mollie's kitchen, idly strok-
ing the old calico cat; he wished he could carry the
fragrance of Miss Mollie's kitchen with him where-
ever he went. Long hours he spent with Grandpa
Bent, whose old eyes sparkled when Timmy told of
the new ships, so big, so swift, so beautiful. The
leave was over all too soon.

The day before he was to go back it rained, dismally. Timmy wandered down to see Parson Meigs; he had grown quite fond of the dusty, faded little man since he came home. He always asked so many questions about Timmy's work, was ever eager to lend him a book.

But Parson Meigs was out; he'd be in soon, Mrs. Meigs thought.

Timmy waited in the queer old shabby study. Two books lay on the table, the big Bible and a slender book of poems. He picked up the poems and settled in one of the worn leather chairs.

> Thou art not what thou wast before,
> What reason I should be the same?

It reminded him of Cissy; he slammed the book and walked to the window. The wind sent lilac blossoms in a shower against the pane. They reminded him of Cissy, too. Only once had he seen her in her lilac-colored gown; he had to admit she looked very lovely but as strange and as far off as his old lucky star he never could be sure of.

He shook his head impatiently. There was no Cissy any more—only a grown-up young lady with dozens of bonnets and beaux.

The wind was rising. Parson Meigs was pretty old to be out in such weather, just to listen to people's troubles; surely, no one would be married on such a day, and babies, with a whole lifetime before them, could well wait to be christened till the sun came out.

Restlessly, he walked back to the desk, sank into the chair, and pulled the open Bible toward him. The page seemed to fade into grayness, nothingness, all save one sentence, clear and strong:

"Thy way is in the sea and thy path in the great waters . . ."

It was getting dark, darker; the room was all shadows now, but through the shadows he saw the glint of sun on blue water, and a boat—his little boat of long ago, her one sail crackling in the wind; he felt the gentle urge of the tiller; then the little sail widened, lengthened, multiplied, sail upon sail, all but brushing Heaven; the tiller tugged harder; it became a great wheel plunging, struggling, under his hands. Down, down, the racking chop of the Atlantic-wind and more wind, blinding, deafening; seas, immense and relentless—this must be the stormy Horn—calm seas again, long, long rollers going on and on—this must be the Pacific . . . .

Timmy rose suddenly from the battered leather of Parson Meigs's old chair and rushed out into the rain.

CHAPTER NINE

THE GULLS ARE CRYING

Uncle Captain, his face going red one minute and white the next, was pounding on Grandpa Bent's door.

"Hold yer horses, Dan," came a voice from within, "I'm comin' fast as I can—I'm an old man. Set down. You look blowed. No—see can you find my specs first and quit shaking that letter under my nose?— if it's Timmy, I never said nothin' to him save how-de-do and good-by, whole time he was home."

His old eyes peered at the letter Uncle Captain laid on the table. Slowly and carefully, he read it aloud.

Hong Kong

Dear Uncle Captain, I'm sorry, but I had to go. Somehow the land got me crazy, one way or another, and no matter how I tried I kept on hearing the sea roaring and the gulls crying. If it wasn't for fear of the hurt to you, and me seeming so ungrateful for the kindness of Mr. Adair, I'd be the happiest man alive. Tell Grandpa Bent, I've seen the red and gold pagodas, and the ladies with little feet, like figures pacing on a fan, and tell Miss Mollie I'm bringing her some tea. And tell Christel whatever music I hear in any land it is always her voice, whether it be the song of the surf on Ceylon, or silver temple bells. Remember me to everybody home, Uncle Captain, and please don't think too hard of me.

Timmy

P. S. I am sending you some money through Mr. Adair's. I will send some regular as I can—I owe you a lot.

"I did all I could," said Uncle Captain wearily.

"And a bit more," said Grandpa Bent. "But don't you come a-blamin' me, Dan; once I knew you was trying to keep him from the sea I held my tongue till I nigh bit through it. You can't blame me, and you can't blame yerself; blame where blame is due—your own secret heart, your own blood and kin, your lost

brother, Timothy, what was his father, and your grandsire, too, and the ones afore him—on and on, back and back, to the first Burney hoisted a sail over the world's rim . . . "

He stopped and looked at Uncle Captain, standing up, very straight and proud.

"You ain't really sorry one mite, Dan," said Grandpa Bent.

And then they both burst out laughing.

~~~~~~

"Cecilia," exclaimed Mrs. Winfield, "where have you been? To Grandpa Bent's, you say? Well, if you don't stop crying you'll never be able to go to that dance. Do you want to go out with pink eyes, like a guinea pig? What on earth is the matter with you?"

There was much the matter—even more than Cissy guessed. It was a long, long time before Timothy Daniel Burney, glittering with the brass buttons of an officer, stepped once more on the brown wharves of home.

"Lord love us," cried Uncle Captain, "how big you are!"

"I'm twenty-one," said Timmy, "and I've sailed all the Seven Seas and I'm first mate of the finest ship that ever—"

"How many of the finest ships there are," said Uncle Captain, and he laughed deep in his throat. "If there's a Heaven for ships—and I've heard tell there is —those golden gates must be wide as all the seas there

are. For, come Judgment Day, every one of them will want to come in under full canvas, and not one an inch behind t'other.

"There'll be Grandpa Bent's ship, and old Captain Dane's, and Michael O'Brian's, and your ship, and," he added, with twinkling eyes, "maybe even my old green fishing dory, with no name to her at all."

"Why," asked Timmy, "is there no name, Uncle Captain?"

"Well, once upon a time there was—and—now there isn't. And even if you are twenty-one, you're far too young to be askin' personal questions of a man some thirty-odd years to the forward of you."

On the whole this had been a wonderful homecoming, with Miss Mollie so excited over her lacquer tea chest, filled with the finest tea in all China, and Grandpa Bent fairly quivering with questions; a visit to the

Vosborgs, where, oh wonder of wonders, in addition to the new pink pigs and colts and calves, there was a baby Christel, and she was none other than Michael O'Brian's and big Christel's together. Though she was too young to sing or say "Eric" (though they had tried to teach her), she could say "red" and she could say "king." Timmy felt every inch a king in his new jacket with the brass buttons, and his heart rose up to choke him when the baby pulled his head down and cooed with delight over his mop of red hair.

~~~~~

"Seen Cissy yet?" inquired Uncle Captain one evening after supper.

"No," said Timmy shortly. Then, in a tone he tried to make very casual, "Thought maybe she'd married and gone away or something."

"Married!" said Uncle Captain, studying Timmy's face through a screen of pipe smoke. "No, indeedy! I figure she's refused about all the young men in seven states by now. Anyways, I think you should go over. Every time I saw Cissy she'd ask about you, and she came over here to listen to every letter you wrote." Suddenly all the bitter feelings in Timmy welled up at once and spilled over.

"There isn't any Cissy any more," he said gruffly.

"The last time I was here there was only a grown-up girl with Cissy's face. And her name is Cecilia. I am not going."

He wondered why he hadn't seen Cissy on the street. The reason was simple: young Miss Winfield, pleading maladies hitherto unknown, had remained strictly at home.

Uncle Captain puffed a long time on his pipe.

"You may be twenty-one, Timmy, and you may have sailed all the Seven Seas and seen all the far places of the globe, but there is still something you've never seen and plenty you've never learned."

Timmy rubbed his brass buttons lovingly. He didn't understand what Uncle Captain meant at all, but he simply couldn't admit it.

"Perhaps," said he.

CHAPTER TEN

HIS OWN FATHER'S SON

Thirteen years ago there had been just such a storm, with murderous, pounding seas and screaming gales and slashing rain. Then there had been a small Timmy shut in the house, and Uncle Captain gone—out yonder. . . .

And now Uncle Captain couldn't go, after that fall he'd had in the autumn, and here was that same Timmy, grown big, jerking on crackling oilskins, and Michael O'Brian waiting for him.

"A schooner, yes, sir," Michael was telling Uncle

Captain, "and it's a mighty poor chance—same old rocks as usual—but we are going to try."

The next minute he and Timmy were gone, with a mighty rush of salty wind and a shower of rain upon the floor.

Uncle Captain stared at the wet pool, at the closed door. He buried his face in his hands.

"Timothy . . ." he murmered, "Timmy. . . ."

But Timmy was already halfway to the wharves.

~~~~~~

Grandpa Bent, bareheaded, stood at his open door, peering forth into the street through a curtain of blinding rain. His old hands trembled on his knobby cane; he was already quite wet, but he must try to catch some passer-by for news.

A huge figure loomed dimly through the grayness.

"Barney, you Barney!" yelled Grandpa Bent.

"Coming, sir!" came an answering bellow.

"Pour me a mite of those sperits there," commanded Grandpa Bent, "and some for yourself—and get on with telling me. It's a wonder someone couldn't get here afore!"

"I run all the way," gasped Little Barney. "I was comin' here afore you hollered. Well, they couldn't get nigh to the rocks in the boats—they would have been tore to kindling wood, so he plunged into that icy water with the ropes—"

"Who? Never mind. I guess I know—"

"Timmy it was—he's his own father's son all right, and no mistake on that—and somehow he got all the men dragged back to the boats. He's got a big gash in his head and is half drowned, but Doctor Petrie says he's got half and half a chance—Grandpa Bent, you can't go out in this rain—you'll take your death—"

"Barney, you run to the smithy and get me a horse, and drag my old carriage out of the barn—what are you standing there for? Don't waste time arguing. I don't care whose horse it is, and I don't care how many shoes it has, on or off, long as the animal has four legs to it! Get me two horses—I can drive faster!"

"But, Grandpa—"

"Who is master of this ship?" yelled Grandpa Bent. His cane lay on the floor; he stood erect, his old eyes flashing.

"Aye aye, Captain Bent," cried Barney, and fled.

~~~~~

Uncle Captain's calloused hands clasped one of the big, limp ones lying on the counterpane.

"Timmy, Timmy," he murmured, over and over, "it's me—it's me—it's Uncle Captain."

"Now, Dan," whispered Doctor Petrie, "don't take on so—he'll come around soon and know you."

And, because he wasn't sure of it at all, he turned away and walked to the window.

"Glory be!" he exclaimed suddenly, "glory, glory be!"

From a creaking carriage, red with rust and green with mold, and drawn by a huge farm horse of Farmer Vosborg's and a skittish saddle horse of Mr. Winfield's, stepped forth, light and quick, Grandpa Bent.

Barney, very red in the face, strove to hold the ill-assorted horses in their odd bits of harness. The rain poured down his face, dripped from his nose and chin unheeded.

The ship's clock struck eight bells and Timmy stirred, opened his eyes.

"Now, Dan, have patience," begged Doctor Petrie.

Timmy's eyes wandered around the room, at the great beams, the nets, the candles burning low, the anxious faces. He didn't seem to be seeing them, but other things.

"The water south," he muttered, "is blue as blue. That's my blue. Oranges grow there, that's my orange—or the cat . . . " his eyes went to the candle flame . . . "yellow . . . the green dory—green . . . "

He was more alert now; he raised a hand to his head.

"My hair, oh, it's all gone!"

Doctor Petrie bent over the bed. "We had to shave it, Tim, to fix that cut on your head."

The blue eyes went groping again, suddenly cleared.

"Doc—Uncle Captain—why, Grandpa Bent!"

He knew them all now.

Tears streamed down Uncle Captain's face as he leaned over the bed.

Timmy raised a hand. "You've been on the wharves again," he murmured; "your face is all wet. You

promised me you'd stay in." He dropped off to sleep again.

Four bells. Timmy spoke again, very low.

"I must get red and violet—I have all the rest."

Cissy's eyes, Cissy's mouth—but he couldn't use them. Besides, they didn't really exist any more; Cissy had gone away. He shook his head and moaned with pain.

Five bells, and he spoke again.

"I must get a red, Uncle Captain." Uncle Captain sighed. If only the boat had come, but she couldn't, he knew, have even started in this storm—the boat with all the Christmas things—holly and red ribbon and apples.

"Don't bother now, Timmy—it's time to sleep— wait till morning."

"No, tonight—it bothers me not to finish the rainbow. Do you suppose Miss Mollie has a red dress? She had most every color."

"I never saw—well, not for years—but we'll ask in the morning."

"No, now—tonight."

"Anything to quiet him," whispered Doctor Petrie, then, as Uncle Captain looked at him pleadingly, he shook his head.

"No, I would not dare leave him now. But—he will live."

"I'm too old to traipse around in the night air," said Grandpa Bent decidedly. "It's up to you, Dan." A flicker of a smile crossed his seamed old face.

Uncle Captain tiptoed softly out.

Across Timmy's long body under the counterpane, the old seaman and the grizzled doctor stared at each other. Long and hard.

CHAPTER ELEVEN

THE RIGHT MAN

The rain had stopped, the moon shone in the wet puddles of the streets, on the darkened houses. Uncle Captain's heavy footsteps echoed loudly in the sleeping town. There was a dim light in the Winfield house, upstairs, in one room. He turned from the street into the lane toward the moors. His footsteps grew slower—yes, there was a light in Miss Mollie's house.

Icy terror gripped Miss Mollie's heart at the knock upon her door. Had someone come to tell her that Timmy—oh, no, it couldn't—it mustn't be!

"Dan!" she cried as she saw Uncle Captain looming in her doorway. "No!"

"No," he said gently, "he is better. Doc just said—he will live."

"Won't you come in, Captain Burney?" It was her fear for Timmy that had made her say "Dan"; her cheeks were pink at the thought of it.

Uncle Captain sat, stiffly, in a gay chintz-covered chair, his dark bulk looking strangely out of place against a pattern of delicate leafage and butterflies and flowers. He spoke very slowly and carefully.

"I didn't expect to come—ever. When you doubted my—my love for you so much that you would not let me help bear the sorrow of your father with you—the burden—when you sent my ring back—I vowed I would never ask you anything again."

"But," cried Miss Mollie, "I wanted you to have happiness without shadows, without any sadness—oh, didn't you understand?"

Her eyes were full of tears.

"I had to come now," he went on doggedly, "for Timmy. It's the rainbow again; he wanted to know if—if, by any chance, you had a red dress?"

With a sudden sob, she was gone. He heard her light

step on the stairs, somewhere above, to and fro—why, almost like dancing.

He turned at the sound of a door, and her voice.

"I'm ready to go, Captain Burney—to Timmy."

Twenty years, twenty long years, all gone in a moment! Here was young Mollie Dane again, in the red dress he had always loved.

"Mollie—" he stumbled toward her—"Mollie!"

"Dan, Dan," protested Miss Mollie, "this dress has been all neat and fresh in tissue paper for twenty—Dan, it would never do for a piece of Timmy's rainbow to be crumpled and mussy!"

~~~~~

"There are times," said Grandpa Bent to Doctor Petrie, "when it would be nice to be a woman, so's you could cry all you want."

~~~~~

For the first time in many weeks, Timmy was able to sit up and enjoy his breakfast. The sun streamed in, striking on the bright orange (Little Barney had run all the way to the wharves and just grabbed it off the boat), on the sparkle of jam, from Miss Mollie, of course, on curling bacon and golden eggs, from the bounty of the Vosborg farm. His heart warmed at the thought of all the kindness.

"What are you doing, Uncle Captain?" he asked, from his throne of many pillows.

"I'm just scratchin' around for a bit of paint, Tim; I'm goin' to put a name on my old green dory."

"What name?"

"Same one it useter have."

"But I never knew what it was; you wouldn't tell me."

Uncle Captain, fumbling among brushes and paint cans, turned very red. But he straightened up and faced Timmy squarely.

"I once told you, young man, there was still plenty

you didn't know. The name was—and will be—the 'Mollie'—the 'Mollie Dane.'"

And all of a sudden, all in a heap, Timmy knew a lot of things.

"Do you suppose," he said at least, "that Grandpa Bent will dance at your wedding?"

Uncle Captain roared.

"I wouldn't put it past him," he said gleefully, "but whatever made you think of that—of Grandpa Bent dancing?"

"Oh, once, a long time ago—" Timmy stopped short. Why had he said that? Why had he even thought of it? Why must everything remind him of Cissy—the little Cissy who had gone away? It was for her wedding Grandpa Bent had promised to dance. Ages and ages ago, before she became Cecilia.

But—he could still see the string of rainbow pearls lying in her small pink palm; see her pansy eyes fixed gravely on Grandpa Bent.

"Oh, wow," he said fretfully, forgetting he was six feet and almost three more inches, and twenty-one, "my head aches again; you know I never did finish that rainbow I started the night I was hurt and had the fever. I never did get a violet. I was so happy when Miss Mollie came, in her red dress, I went to sleep."

Timmy walked slowly down the street. Pansies in every garden—tulips of all colors—lilacs everywhere. But Timmy, somehow, didn't feel like making a rainbow. He missed his ship terrible—no, terribly—with the long swells below and the wheeling gulls above. But Doc had been very firm.

"Not till autumn, Tim, not till autumn."

He turned in at Grandpa Bent's and knocked, tenderly lifting the brass anchor of the door knocker.

"Well, well, and well, Timmy, to think I'm still a-settin' here, making little ships same as I did when your head bare topped this table, and now I'm half skeered you'll butt my ceiling down any day. Some things change a lot, and others not at all."

"Do you think I've changed?"

"Only in pounds and inches and such. Underneath

you're the same you was, always. I never saw anyone change less, except maybe Cissy Winfield."

Timmy glared.

"She has changed. She's not even Cissy any more; she's just a strange grown-up girl named Cecilia. Perhaps I ought to say Miss Winfield."

"Well, well, and we-l-l," said Grandpa Bent slowly. "I hadn't noticed it. But I guess I'm gettin' old and don't see good any more. Why, yesterday when she was here I couldn't believe she wasn't the selfsame little girl with yeller curls—and what do you reckon she wanted? Why, to look at my red dragon chest and the blue slipper—hello, here's Mollie—Mollie, was Cissy over to your house yesterday, inquiring for anything?"

"She was, Captain—yellow tulips; and I'd taken every one over to the church. She had to use the canary again— Oh, dear, deary me, what made Timmy dash off like that? What on earth did I say?"

"Great sun, moon, and stars, Marse Tim! Hallelujah, boy, I couldn't get the door open no faster! Yes, she's home—she's in the garden."

Happily, widely grinning, big Caesar peered from the shelter of a window curtain as Timmy plunged down the garden walk.

Cissy, sitting on the grass, jumped to her feet when she heard a man's running footsteps.

"Timothy—you—what on earth is the matter?"

In one hand he held an orange tulip, in the other a handful of grass. He was bareheaded and breathless, and his face was almost as red as his hair. He looked so utterly ridiculous Cissy laughed, hysterically. He didn't seem to notice.

"Orange and green," he stammered, "and you have on a blue dress, and—and—may I have your hair for yellow? And your eyes again for violet?"

Cissy, choking down sobs and battling tears, could only nod. A great comb fell on the grass and all her curls tumbled around her face.

Timmy slipped a brown finger under her trembling chin.

"Look at me, Cissy," he said. "Can I—I mean may I—also have your mouth for red? Please."

"Yes, I know," said Uncle Captain. "I knew when I saw you coming, Tim, so don't waste your breath —save it so's to run to Grandpa Bent's and tell him afore somebody else does."

~~~~

"Well, well, and we-l-l," said Grandpa Bent, "I thought you was another storm comin,' Tim. . . . You don't tell me! . . . No! Of course I never guessed! But I'm not a-sayin' I didn't hope!"

His eyes sparkled. He opened the cupboard, took out the lacquer box—and pale rainbows shone in the pearls upon the table.

"Now, Tim, ketch your breath, and then run an errand for me."

"They are for—Cissy?"

"And who else? Don't you remember what I said?" He lifted a gnarled forefinger.

"A sailor, first and last, a big man and a brave one, and—he must dream dreams! Now that's you to a tee, Timmy, every bit of it!"

"But," cried Timmy, "you should give them to her yourself."

"No— and agin no. I'm gettin' old, and I got to save up all my strength."

"For what?"

"Boy, boy," said Grandpa Bent, "have ye no memory at all? Why, to dance at the wedding!"